Words by
Jordan Scott

Pictures by
Sydney Smith

I TALK
LIKE A
RIVER

WALKER BOOKS

I wake up

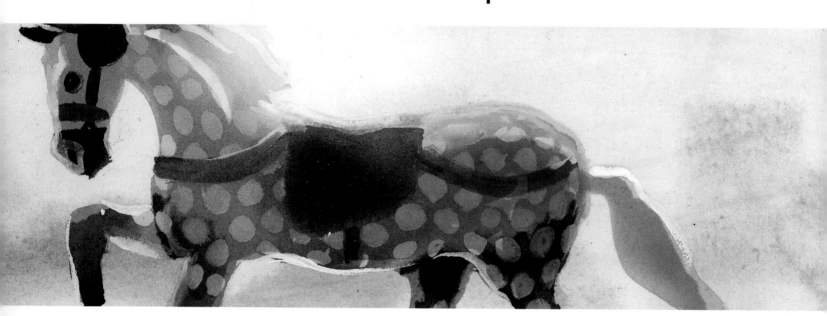

with the sounds of words

each morning

all around me.

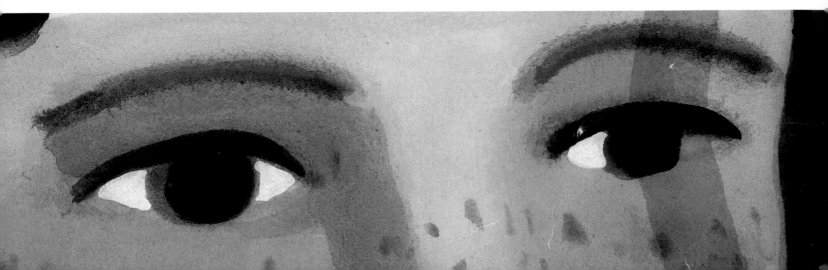

P for the pine tree outside my
bedroom window.

C for the crow in its branches.

M for the moon fading in
the morning sky.

I wake up each morning
with the sounds of words
all around me.

And I can't say them all.

The P
  in pine tree
    grows roots
  inside my mouth
and tangles
  my tongue.

The C is a crow
  that sticks
    in the back
  of my throat.

The M in moon
  dusts my lips
    with a magic
      that makes me
    only mumble.

I wake up in the
morning with these
word-sounds stuck
in my mouth.

I stay quiet
as a stone.

I eat my porridge without a peep.
I get ready for the day without a word.

At school, I hide in the back of class.
I hope I don't have to talk.

When my teacher asks me a question,
all my classmates turn and look.

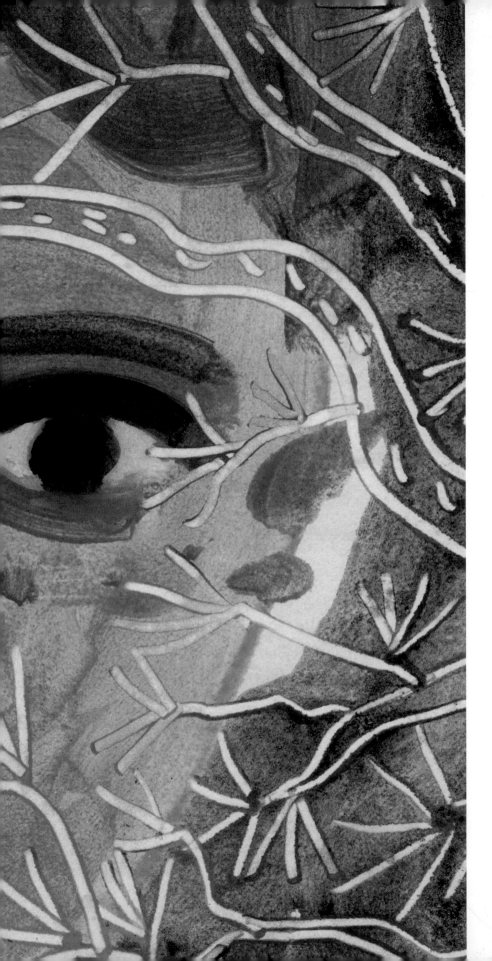

They don't see
  a pine tree sticking
    out from my lips
instead of
  a tongue.

They don't hear
  a crow *Caw! Caw!*
    from inside
      my throat.

They don't hide
  their eyes from
    the moonlight
    that shines from
my open mouth.

All they hear is how I don't talk like them.
All they see is how strange my face looks
and that I can't hide how scared I am.

My mouth isn't working.
It's full with words
of the morning.

Mornings are always
hard, but this one's
especially tough.
I'm more stuck
than ever.

My teacher says
we all have to talk
about our
favourite place
in the world.

Today is my turn
but my mouth
just isn't working,
and I want to go home.

My dad picks me up from school.
"It's just a bad speech day," he says.
"Let's go somewhere quiet."

My dad takes me to the river.

We walk along the shore looking for colourful rocks and water bugs.

It feels good to be quiet
and alone with my dad.

But I can't stop thinking
about my bad speech day:

All those eyes watching
  my lips
      twist and twirl,

all those mouths
      giggling
   and laughing.

I feel a storm in my belly;
my eyes fill with rain.

My dad sees I am sad and pulls me
close; he points to the river and says:

"See how that water moves?
That's how you speak."

I look at the water

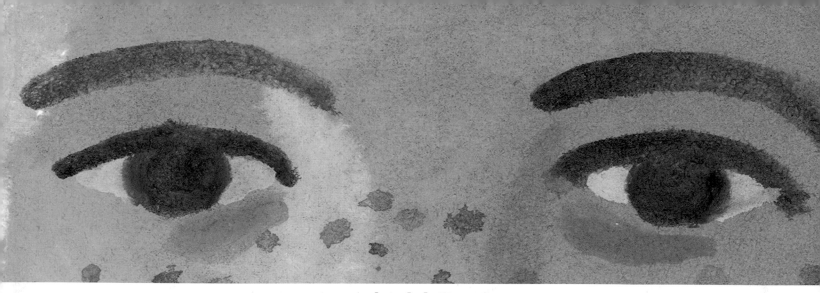

bubbling,

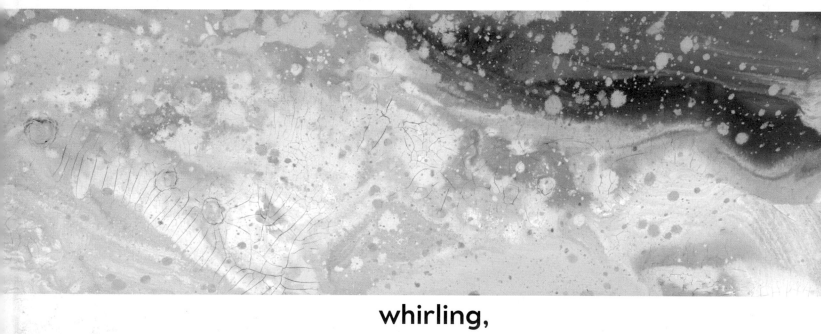

whirling,

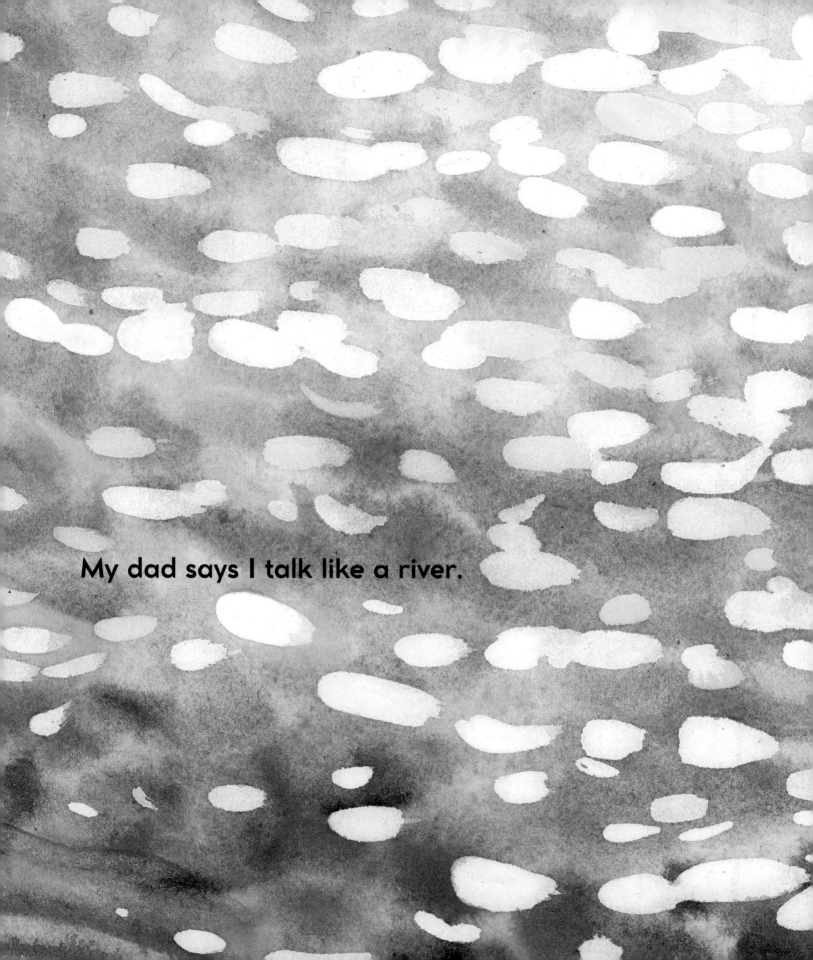

My dad says I talk like a river.

churning,

and crashing.

This is what I like to remember,
to help stop myself from crying

I talk like a river

or from not wanting to speak at all.

I talk like a river

When the words around me are hard to say, I think of the proud river,

bubbling,

churning,

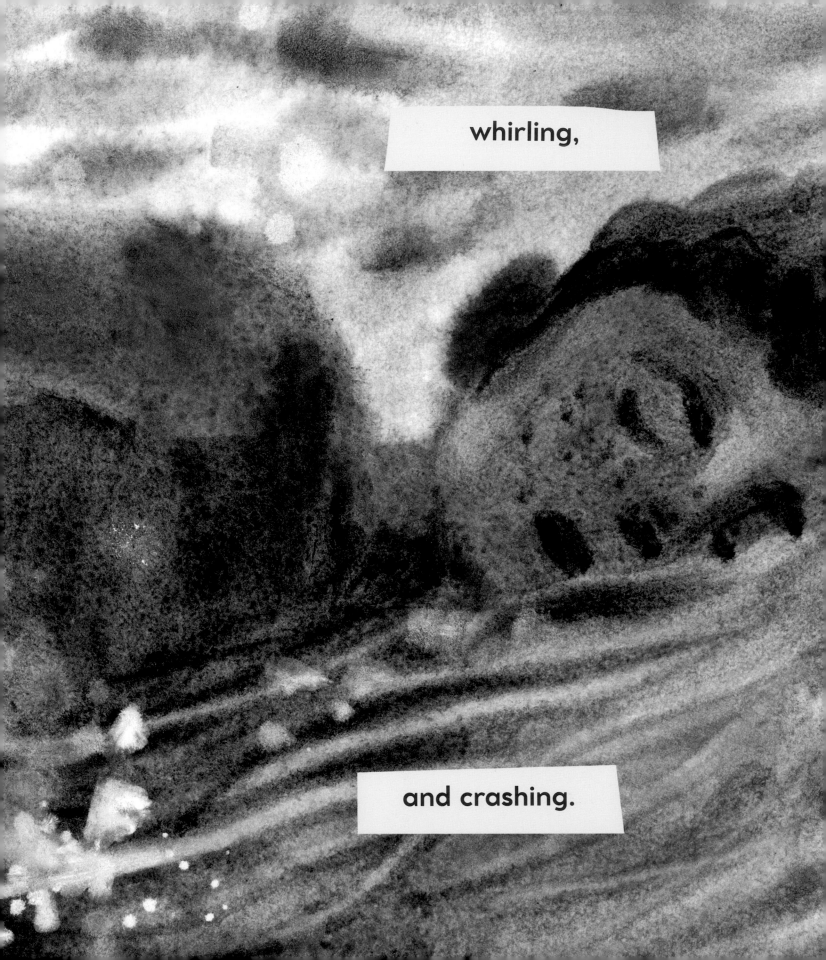

whirling,

and crashing.

And I also think of the calm river beyond the rapids where the water is smooth and glistening.

This is how my mouth moves.

This is how I speak.

Even the river stutters.

Like I do.

I wake up in the morning
  with the sounds of words
all around me.

I go to school and tell the class about my favourite place in the world.

I talk about the river.

And I talk like a river.

How I Speak

When I was a boy my dad would sometimes pick me up from school on "bad speech days" and take me down to the river. On those days my mouth would just stop working. Every word was painful; the laughter from classmates unbearable. I just wanted to be quiet. Along the river we skipped stones, watched for salmon, picked up bugs, and plucked blackberries, all without saying a word.

One particular day, while watching the water move against the shore, my dad said: "You see how that water moves, son? That's how you speak."

Stuttering is often mocked because it is seen as unnatural. For many, listening to and watching someone stutter is not a comfortable experience because language and sound are stretched to their limits. Strange noises burst from a contorting mouth, and what the listener thinks of as fluency or "normal speech" explodes. To stutter is to be dysfluent; and fluency, my speech therapist used to say, is the ultimate goal.

But at the river, I learned to think differently about fluency. The river has a mouth, a confluence, a flow. The river is a natural and patient form, forever making its way toward something greater than itself. Yet as the river moves, it stutters, and I do too.

Take a moment to listen to the way you talk. How do you sound? What would happen if you concentrated on the feeling of speaking? Where do you feel words in your body? Do you speak without pauses or hesitations? How often do you slip up, forget words, or have difficulty finding them in the first place? Do you sometimes shy away from speaking? Do you sometimes not want to say anything at all?

My dad took me to the river so I would feel less alone. When he pointed to the river, he gave image and language to talk about something so private and terrifying. In doing so, he connected my stuttering to the movements of the natural world and I delighted in watching my mouth move outside of itself.

Everyone who stutters does so differently. A stutter is never just a stutter but a set of intricately intimate labours with words, sound, and body. My stutter is my own and also part of a larger confluence of dysfluent mouths going about their day: ordering food at a restaurant, making small talk about the weather, or talking to loved ones. Stuttering makes me feel profoundly connected and profoundly alone. Stuttering is terrifyingly beautiful. Sometimes I want to speak without worrying; sometimes I want to speak with grace, finesse, and with all those words you can think of for smooth. But that is not me.

I talk like a river.

—J.S.

This book is for my father, Roy Scott—J.S.

To my son, Salvador—S.S.

I Talk Like a River would not have been possible without
the friendship, wisdom, and editorial brilliance of Lara LeMoal.

I would like to thank Hilary McMahon for believing in me and this story.
I would also like to thank Sydney Smith for his remarkable illustrations and
Neal Porter for his incomparable vision in bringing this work to life.

Thanks to Anuj Parikh for helping to craft the last lines,
somewhere in Guanajuato.

As always, love to my mom, Wiesia Kujawa, for giving me the gift of poetry;
and to my family, Summer, Rowan, and Sacha, for giving me the gift to go on.

—J.S.

First published in the UK 2021 by Walker Books Ltd
87 Vauxhall Walk, London SE11 5HJ

This edition published 2022

2 4 6 8 10 9 7 5 3 1

Text © 2020 Jordan Scott
Illustrations © 2020 Sydney Smith

First published in the United States 2020 by Neal Porter Books, Holiday House
Publishing, Inc. Published by arrangement with Holiday House Books, New York

The right of Jordan Scott and Sydney Smith to be identified as the author
and illustrator respectively of this work has been asserted by them in
accordance with the Copyright, Designs and Patents Act 1988

This book has been typeset in Cocomat Pro Bold

Printed in China

British Library Cataloguing in Publication Data:
a catalogue record for this book is available from the British Library

ISBN 978-1-5295-0281-7

www.walker.co.uk